MODERN MANIA

KOFI M KRAMO

Order this book online at www.trafford.com
or email orders@trafford.com

Most Trafford titles are also available at major online book retailers.

Print information available on the last page.

ISBN: 978-1-4907-8960-6 (sc)
ISBN: 978-1-4907-8961-3 (e)

Trafford rev. 08/09/2018

www.trafford.com
North America & international
toll-free: 1 888 232 4444 (USA & Canada)
fax: 812 355 4082

To
My family

SUSPENDED GLASS FOOTPATHS

1

M Y EYES WEREN'T quite in tune with THAT darkness. THAT darkness which channels your body and mind through to sleep. Not normal darkness. Normal darkness still lets you see the outline of a wardrobe, a door that rests ajar, the speckled projection of light seeping through a gap in the curtains. THAT darkness was fuzzy, but at the same time it was dense. My inability to see my transitional blackness wasn't the only factor preventing sleep. I struggled to get my right arm comfortable – it felt like an awkward third arm. I finally started to drift off to sleep when the phone rang. I reached for the phone and answered it with a croaky hello. I was met with background noise. I heard disjointed shouting and the sound of objects smashing. Then I heard a voice.

"Adrian Sarpong, you there? Can you hear me?"

"Yes, who's this?"

"It's Kate"

"Hi Kate, what's going on there, you ok?"

"Did you know?"

"Know what?"

"Don't protect him. Did you know?"

"Know what, Kate?"

She slammed the phone down before I could respond. I sat in the darkness with the receiver, still by my ear, emitting a dead tone. Twenty minutes later, the phone rang again. It was my best friend Al. He apologised to me for his wife's angry phone call. He then provided the context. It involved a woman from New York who he'd been chatting to online for the past 6 months. He'd become obsessed with her, transforming her onscreen words into images in his mind of a woman who was intelligent, witty and alluring. He'd wanted to abandon everything and be with her. The possibility of a physical union took a step closer 2 months into their virtual discourse, when she'd sent Al a message saying that she was in Europe after booking a last minute holiday. Stockholm to be precise but soon leaving for Vienna. She'd implored Al to join her. She'd recommended an online travel company called Project Utopia that, she told him, was reasonably priced and offered an all-inclusive hotel and flight package. Al subsequently booked through Project Utopia and told Kate that he was going to Vienna on business. When he'd arrived in Vienna, he made his way to the Schönbrunn Palace, where they'd arranged to meet for the first time. After a couple of hours exploring the gardens and decorative palace interior, alone, breaking for a lunch of wiener schnitzel and salad, Al reluctantly came to the conclusion that he'd been stood up for whatever reason. He tried in vain to email her when he finally checked in to the hotel but he'd received no response. He had returned to London confused, telling Kate more lies to explain why his business trip had ended abruptly.

It was by chance that 2 months later a bout of insomnia drew Al's blurry eyes to the harsh reality of what really happened to him in Vienna. A late night news programme showed an investigative journalist hounding a couple of men with coats over their heads. They were purportedly directors of Sun, Sea and Purity Travel. The journalist was loudly asking the panicked directors why their travel agents were operating fake dating websites. Luring unsuspecting people into long distance relationships, dangling Sun, Sea and Purity flight and hotel products in front of their besotted victims − offering the chance to see distant lovers in the flesh. Al didn't want to believe he had fallen victim to the scam until the investigative journalist mentioned Sun, Sea and Purity Travel was also the parent company of Pop Holiday Travel and Project Utopia.

Al had the feeling of his heart tumbling down like a heavy bolder. After sitting for a while in the dark, passively allowing his eyes to consume the rays of light from the TV, the shame metamorphosed into a burning desire to seek justice and made confessing his indiscretion to Kate an easy decision. He wanted a clear path to pursue the con artists through the courts. Al explained to me that Kate had phoned to find out whether I had been complicit − she wanted to know how extensive her humiliation would be. When Al finished speaking, he refused to hear my thoughts on the whole affair. He simply said goodnight in a low voice and, for the second time that night, the phone to my ear emitted a dead tone.

Observation number: 234

> *Crisp leaves rested on the newly laid concrete pavement slabs. The leaves had a dyed effect – a pallid brown running into green – and marks that looked like a coin had been used to lightly scratch at their surfaces.*

This was my job: observing and making notes on things like leaves on concrete. Other jobs require people to brainstorm –discuss ideas around a table, represent thoughts pictorially before deciding on a firm plan of action. The beauty of my work was that I didn't actually have to come up with a plan of action. I simply wrote about what I saw, anything that interested me. My official job title was Community Observer. I worked for the Mayor of London in his Design and Development Agency located away from City Hall, in Camden Town. Once I'd gathered a day's worth of observations, I would submit my notes to the Agency's creative directors, Anton Dex and Christian Foster. They would decide whether my notes could inspire designers and architects in the Agency by revealing what was lacking or desired in the capital. Previously my notes had inspired the design of prototypes such as an innovative waste bin for London high streets, and a new type of energy-saving street lamp. However, although the Mayor's Agency had bravely created products from my random thoughts, the product designs hadn't stretched technological capabilities, nor had they shown much creativity. Instead of breaking through the wall to see what was on the other side, it seemed much easier to paint the wall a different colour. I wasn't overly impressed that my thoughts, words, were leading to prosaic designs and products.

It was late in the evening when I got back to the office – a modern, open-planned workspace with glass meeting rooms scattered around five floors. I put my notes on the desk and proudly read through them before typing them up. Later that night Al rang when I was sitting on the sofa in my flat off Holloway Road. He'd spent the whole day drinking in bar. His speech was slurred to such an extent that I couldn't understand large segments of what he was saying, but at the heart of his drivel was a lament about his lost cyber-woman. I allowed him to vent for 10 minutes before finding a way to end the call.

Alex Perkins and I had been friends since secondary school. We'd come together because of a shared interest: rivals in pursuit of the school beauty, Marina Echo. Having both failed in our attempts to woo her, we ended up mourning her together at each other's houses. We grew closer mainly because Al had a real craving for my mum's jollof rice. His appreciation of Ghanaian cuisine ensured that he had an open invitation to my house. Our friendship was confirmed when we realised we shared the same taste in music. We would chill out at his house listening to records by artists such as Sharon Clarke and the Product of Time, Sam Cooke and Donny Hathaway. We would often talk about how silly it was that we had chased the same girl. We referred to that period as *The Race for Marina*. We would recall how we had kept our distance from one another, not sharing too much information, because we'd been scared that knowing too much about your rival would somehow play into their hands and allow them to steal a march in the race. Al having not told me about this cyber-woman from the start took me back to those school days. He was acting as if he was conditioned not to tell me too much information about his love life.

2

CARDBOARD BOXES WERE ubiquitous. They were stacked together, flattened, half opened or half destroyed. The store's customers weren't repelled by this warehouse vibe created by the boxes. They happily sought out stereo separates, camcorders, tumble dryers and vacuum cleaners, without commenting on the mess. People frantically climbed over boxes, batted them aside with the back of their hands or crunched them down with their shoes – leaving dirty imprints. This was Eric Constanopolis' store at the Islington end of Seven Sisters Road, lodged between a discount *bric-a-brac* outlet and a fishmonger. I'd been a regular at Eric's electrical store, not because I was attracted to his products (they had the propensity to be faulty) but because of Eric's character. He had wit, an opinion on all subjects. The first time I visited his store, I forgot what I was there to buy after he approached me, sucked me in with his charismatic personality. We struck up a friendship and I often went to see him for light entertainment.

"Adrian, you buying something or come to see me?"

"I've come to browse and see you of course."

"It's a good day, I received delivery of some real cutting-edge stock."

"Word must have spread: I've never seen it so busy in here."

"I got all the latest TVs. Massive plasmas, the best portables and TVs complete with surround-sound systems. Better than the cinema!"

"But you're still selling us TVs."

"Of course."

"The media-viewing concept hasn't changed."

"What you mean?"

Eric stared at me as if he'd suddenly become suspicious. I continued to tell him how the world was stuck in a television design loop, that no one seemed to be breaking down barriers to create something new. Al countered my argument by telling me how technology was changing the look and feel of TVs. He argued that traditional TVs were bulky and full of vacuum tubes, but that now plasma TVs use gases, which reduce the depth of modern TVs, allowing for fresh designs and in truth creating a new product. I still wasn't convinced.

"The TV may be sandpapered around the edges, made more oval and flatter, but it still hasn't shifted that much from being a square image. It's a designing conspiracy."

"You're talking crazy", Eric replied.

"Why aren't we viewing holograms, emanating from projector pods? Why are we still constrained by boxed images?"

Eric always wore his tie casually, loose, with the top button of his shirt undone. He aimed to portray a business look with a hint of working-class graft. He was wearing light colours to contrast with his thick black hair. His suspicious look suddenly turned to one of certainty: a look he would give to someone that he was absolutely sure was about to shoplift.

"I've no time for this. I've got to serve customers who still appreciate good TVs" Eric replied, as he threw an empty cardboard box over the cashier's desk.

Avril Diamond arrived at my house at 9pm. Her black face was covered in coconut butter, which shined like a thoroughly polished bronze bust. Hair extensions draped to below her shoulders: the ends were singed by a lighter or matches to create a tidy finish. I took her coat, bottle of red wine and walnut bread she'd brought to accompany my palm oil and sea bream soup. Avril and I had been going out for 3 months. We'd met at work. She held a more conventional job within the Mayor's Design and Development Agency — as an architect. We ate the soup tentatively, after 3 months we were still in a coy period, not a time for slurping and spilling. I never used napkins at dinner, but ostentatiously there it was, immaculately laid across my thighs. I secretly wanted her to break and totally lose it, by letting out a burp or smudging her lipstick to reveal her nervousness around me. But she didn't. Her hands were steady, her lips were parted and the spoon successfully transported the soup into her mouth without spillage — every time.

Her eyes had a sparkle, which told me: *You can't catch me out. I've done this kind of thing a thousand times.* We moved our soup bowls into the centre of the table and started on the wine. We joked about corkscrews, how when you are on your own the cork comes out in one piece – the wine is never corked. I offered her more wine. We laughed as two pieces of cork came rolling through the bottle and partially obstructed the flow of wine from the bottle to the glass.

"Lovely soup, just how I like it – nice and strong", said Avril.

"Glad you appreciate my sweat and tears."

"Sorry I was late. I'm working on this exciting project with Anton, so I was held up."

"What's the project?"

"You were the inspiration."

"I was?"

"Yes. Anton read your observation notes on concrete slabs and autumn leaves – he came up with this fantastic idea."

Avril said wiping her full lips with a blue napkin.

"What's the idea?", I asked.

Avril retrieved her cream corduroy handbag from the sofa and took out some rough sketches.

"What are these?", I asked, trying to concentrate my stare, as the wine started to take effect.

"These are suspended glass footpaths."

"Footpaths?"

Avril went on to explain that Anton had brought a psychologist to the office, to analyse my notes on concrete pavements and leaves in more detail. The psychologist had concluded that I was trying to say London pedestrians were depressed because the ground they walk on is hard concrete covered in litter, which turns some disillusioned youngsters to crime. Avril was then tasked with leading a project group to see whether they could design something to tackle the issue. They decided that the wasteland in Camden, which was to be turned into a new shopping village with a road dissecting the west and east side of the village, would have suspended glass footpaths to link the two sides of the complex. The ground level would be for cars only. The light-reflecting footpaths would lift the spirits of visiting shoppers: the footpaths would provide an antidote to depression and criminal tendencies. Avril looked up from the designs and patiently waited for me to respond. I stretched open my dull-brown eyes and raised my glass.

"Sounds great."

Internally I was suffering, I wondered whether I had landed myself with an architect clone. Maybe I had wrongly thought that Avril was a designer who didn't want to deceive the world, someone who had integrity. In truth, maybe she was part of the bizarre culture of holding back progress. I had to convince myself that Avril was genuinely trying to produce something that would be revolutionary and not just designing glorified bridges – I liked her too much to be principled about my principles. I started telling myself that Avril envisaged a London that had a network of suspended glass footpaths that would replace concrete pavement – a city design where people would walk around suspended on glass, able to see both below and above.

3

M Y GREAT TASK was to surmount 700 pages of fiction. I'd read a review in the paper about the book, which said it was for earnest readers only. When I purchased the novel the sheer size of it was daunting. I knew I had to be brave and just attack it. I'd started reading the opening chapters several times because there was always a distraction that sullied my memory of the beginning. I regularly put the manuscript somewhere central – the kitchen table or on the bed – as a constant reminder that it was there. I fooled myself by thinking that I could finish the book within a couple of days if I wanted to. In my mind I would draw up reading timetables. When the time came to read, I would have one too many television programmes to watch. It was impossible for me to achieve silence, but that was exactly what I needed for reading. I couldn't read with the stereo on, as the words on the page would convert into the words of Gil Scott-Heron or Curtis Mayfield and suddenly I would be singing and my concentration would dissolve. But I never sacrificed the stereo. An air of assiduity suddenly fell upon me and I started reading. Five pages into the book, with Mayfield's *Pusherman* playing loudly in the background, I stopped.

Just before midday, I considered two possible plans for the afternoon – persevere with the tome or visit Al. I decided on the latter, to see Al face to face – hear more about his current situation and check his emotional state. I arrived at his parents' house in the late afternoon. Al was pleased to see me, but on the way to the local pub he asked again why he couldn't stay at my place while planning for his future. I wasn't able to give him an answer. Maybe, subconsciously, in some cobwebbed corner of my brain, a lingering evil streak from *The Race for Marina* was affecting my decision. We arrived at the Marquis of Granby and made our way to the beer garden, taking advantage of the sun which shone in resistance to the gathering dark clouds. After half an hour the dark clouds finally overpowered the sun, so we moved inside. The interior of the Marquis of Granby didn't allow light to filter through effectively and the sombre ambience impacted on Al, bringing all his troubles to the surface. He rubbed his forehead with one hand. I put my hand on his shoulder and started to shake him.

"It's not that bad, trust me. Kate will be back."

The alcohol had given me courage to speak defiantly in Al's favour even though I knew Kate was a very fiery, contumacious person.

"I'm not struggling because of Kate, It's that internet thing. The girl not being real!"

"Really!", I said in disgust.

"I opened myself up completely. It's an intrusion."

"You'll get compensation out of the scandal and no doubt there will be prosecutions, I'm sure of that", I said in an attempt to lift his spirits.

We ordered more beer and a small basket of potato wedges. Al picked up a potato and, holding it between his finger and thumb, he started to study it in great detail. His eyes were a whirl of grey and green: the two colours fighting for dominance in his iris but were unable to successfully merge and create a hybrid colour. His concentration was so intense that his lower lip dropped, revealing the slight gap between his two central lower teeth. Al was a thin man and the clothes he wore were a constant reminder of that fact. They pressed themselves tightly around him, clearly defining his shoulder blades, elbows and knee caps.

"I think I'm going to travel with my compensation – leave the fraud department of Funky Fones", Al said in a somewhat distorted manner because the mushed potato he was eating was hot on his tongue.

"I haven't cracked enough jokes about the irony" I said, laughing.

"It shows that my job hasn't made me cynical or paranoid. Can you say the same thing?"

"Cynical maybe, paranoia is a state of mind belonging to the last century – pre-digital."

"I won't even ask what that means, but okay you're cynical about design innovation – don't know why it gets to you so much".

"We are blatantly being tricked. Tricked into believing that the world has changed by putting bigger wheels and a new metallic spray on a car and calling it a revolutionary new model. Cars have been around for 100 years – who gives a shit about cars, tell me who?"

"Everyone."

"Exactly! We're people of the 21st century and we're still talking about cars. Not hover-carts or wall-trams – the technology is there." I said. Al pointed out that some things weren't practical and how expensive it would be to implement my radical ideas on travel. Al seemed to have fully embraced the discussion and was now upbeat. Cyber-woman was temporarily out of his thoughts.

We drank for another hour before ending our drunken, amateurish discussion.

4

B ATTER RAN INTO the pan on the mobile stove
before it solidified, puffed-up and became
pancake. It was tossed and put on a plate and sprinkled
with sugar and lemon drops, before being served to
Martin from IT support. Andrea sipped her orange
juice and talked to Troy, who drank sparkling wine
from a champagne flute. Two administrative officers
passed them, wheeling a projector on a trolley into
the lift and safely to the storage area in the basement
of the building. Avril fiddled with the light dimmer
switch in the main meeting room – increasing the
light output – as people continued to pile out of the
meeting room into the open-plan common workspace,
where the reception was being held. It was 8.45am
and the office was vibrant: the catering team provided
plenty of food and drink. Mayor Greenwood was in
the centre of the office, desperately trying to listen
to three different conversations. The reception
followed a crucial meeting between the Mayor and
his Design Agency. The Mayor had previously agreed
to the suspended glass footpaths. The meeting was an

opportunity for Avril to present the final scaled model. She wore a translucent black satin dress with sequins (a niggling voice in my head was saying her dress was a bit too much for work, but I silenced it). I tried to go towards her, but the Mayor swerved around a few people, directly into her path. The material on Avril's dress looked like a series of small water currents, as his hand made its way down her back and settled on her buttocks. He distracted Avril from his lingering hand by talking shop.

"Marvellous. It truly is", he said as he continued to talk about how the glass structures moved away from gloomy concrete paths, which were said to contribute to social disorder such as vandalism and street crime. He acknowledged that concrete, in conjunction with the horrible English weather, created a mood of discontent. Mayor Greenwood was wearing a pale-green tweed blazer, his eyes were bloodshot and the bags beneath them were well established. He smelt of whisky and sweat. Avril nodded in agreement with everything he said.

"It's the best project I've been involved with to date. I'm so excited about these footpaths."

As I heard Avril say this, I panicked. I dashed over.

"Actually it's a blueprint for a city-wide network of suspended walking – on glass."

Mayor Greenwood looked at me as if I had a potent smell. He lowered his bottom lip and screwed up his nose.

"And you are?"

"I'm Adrian Sarpong. I work here. I'm the person who made the report about leaves on concrete, which led to Anton setting up the design brief that subsequently led to Avril's design."

"So you're the boy who knows the friend of the superstar", he said laughing, as he moved off to blend in with another small group of people.

I could feel Avril's eyes on the back of my head. I turned and faced her. I wanted people to know that she had a creative mind and that she was more than just a bridge builder. I wanted her to be a revolutionary architect. I believed that all architects should deal in restoration or revolution.

"You're embarrassing me. What's this rubbish about a city network? You're confusing the Major after I've just presented the real vision to him."

"I'm sorry. Go mingle – enjoy the reception. You deserve it."

I watched her glide back into the crowd. She looked back at me, sternly, warning me not to cause any more problems. I put on my trench coat and left the office to start my day jotting down observations.

5

I OPENED THE NOVEL approximately at the centre pages then I gripped the page edges, on both sides, bending the book to crease the spine. I wanted to make it look worn and to lose its tidiness – to erase its sense of being a monument. I wanted to turn the book into a pragmatic tool that didn't seem like a stranger to touch –– to cover it with fingerprints and spilt liquid and to bend the tips of the pages. I started reading rapidly. The text enticed me as I'd reached a section with notions I was familiar with and flowing syntactical structures, which spurred me on to page 110. I was satisfied that I'd put a reasonable dent into reading the novel that, in some ways, I feared. I was reading in Finsbury Park on a cold Saturday. The park was somewhat deserted. Sporadic joggers bounced along, breathing out frosty, cloudy air. I looked out, peering through the gaps in the criss-crossed park fence, to Seven Sisters Road. The main road was equally deserted, just the occasional bus shooting by. I felt a vibration and removed my mobile from my coat pocket. It was Al ringing me from a Cardiff conference entitled: *One step ahead of phone fraud.*

"I've seen her!"

"Who?"

"Internet girl", Al said in a secretive tone.

"Get a grip."

"It sounds silly I know, but this lady here – one of the speakers … speaking right now. She is exactly how I imagined internet girl to be. The way she speaks, her figure and humour: it all matches."

"Instead of you sorting out a once happy marriage, you're chasing fiction – the make believe."

"She keeps looking over."

"Probably because you're on the phone and she thinks it's rude – seeing as she's delivering a lecture."

"It's not that kind of a look."

"I'm hanging up."

"I have to introduce myself at the coffee interval."

"I'm hanging up now."

"Adrian"

"Goodbye."

I went swimming that afternoon, allowing the chlorine to burn my eyes. I started some lung-bursting laps, which I hadn't attempted in 4 years. My belly slightly overlapped my swimming shorts – I was nervous at first, but I overcame my initial apprehension. I'd been told that swimming is a full work out, all-inclusive, complete. I felt light and hungry when I pressed my hands down on the side of the pool and lifted my body out.

6

> *The bus is ugly with its screwed-up front and industrial grill. The panel of glass imprisons the driver, who handles the wheel like a competitive sailing team — tacking and jibing. The entrance is the exit — simply an open space that allows chancers to jump off as the bus is in motion. The conductor is seemingly in a marketplace bellowing orders — 'tickets please' and 'take a seat at the front or upstairs'. The bus is red and, even when it is dirty, the red seems to provoke the city and tourists who zealously snap away at it.*

I WAS IN LONDON'S West End, writing my notes for the Agency. I sat on the upper deck of the Routemaster, by the window. An elderly lady sat next to me. She didn't distinguish between the seat fabric and my coat fabric — she freely invaded my personal space without bearing me in mind. I felt like an accessory – her handbag squashed in the corner. After giving the lady an accusative glance, I returned to writing in my notepad.

"What you writing my dear?", the lady said after deciding both to notice my existence and to take an interest in what I was doing. I was slightly irked at her intrusive questioning.

"Nothing much."

"You a poet? Very poetic description of this bus."

She continued, loudly.

"It's work, my job."

"You a reporter?

I asked the lady whether I could be excused and then I moved to sit downstairs. A seat was free. I sat by the window and watched trees, cars and people flash by. I became so engrossed that I didn't feel the body that sat next to me. It was a while before I heard the soft murmur of my name and a light poke on my shoulder. It was Kate. She looked fragile: there was an element of translucency about her. Subcutaneous blues, purples and reds were seeping through her eyelids, through the rings under her eyes, and through her ears and cheeks. Her usually thick, bobbed brown hair looked wiry and spacious like an autumn tree.

"How are you Adrian?", she asked me in a happy voice.

"Good, real good", I said.

I didn't know whether she actually wanted me to answer.

"And yourself, how you keeping?" I asked, cringing at what was flagrantly a stupid question. Kate seemed to drift over my question and she landed the conversation at a point much further down the line from where it had started.

"Honestly, did you know about the affair?"

"It would be hard to categorise it as such."

"Just tell me!" Kate said, loudly enough to turn some heads.

"Ok, take it easy. I found out about the affair at the same time you did. The night you rang me."

"What do you think about the whole thing?"

"I think he is sorry for hurting you."

"Really?"

"He's in denial at the moment" I said, expecting her to swear, scream, cry and say I was lying, as being in denial really meant that he didn't give a shit. But she calmly, philosophically, replied by saying people profess that the internet draws everyone closer. In reality it makes us more distant. Kate then got up from her seat to leave at an awkward time, when the bus was turning. I told her that I'd have a word with Al and see if he'd make time to see her, to work things out. Kate acted as if she couldn't hear me and continued to exit the bus.

7

E RIC BROUGHT PACITA De La Cruz across the
shop floor, to the 'home security zone', where I was
looking at the latest security cameras. Pacita had long,
layered black hair. She towered over Eric in high heels
and wore tapered grey trousers and zipped-up black mac.

"My passion is entertainment products. Don't
know why I've started selling home security gadgets –
I blame my accountant." Eric said scratching part of
neck exposed by his open top shirt button.

"You text me, what's urgent?", I said.

"I got a random email from someone in El
Salvador asking whether I supply spy equipment. He
must be spamming electrical stores all over the globe."

"That's what you wanted to tell me?"

Eric continued to tell how the El Salvadorian
offered him an amount of money that he could retire
on. Eric pointed out that he might be Greek but he
wouldn't sell things that could be turned against this
country.

"I'm not like the Conservative fools who
sanctioned those super gun parts and who knows

what else. I don't even stock the things he wants. He probably needs to contact MI5."

Pacita was nodding supportively. I looked at her, she noticed and stopped nodding – realising that she was giving the impression of being a sycophant. I then looked curiously at Eric. It was irritating that, having put something in his head, he wouldn't rest until he had an answer. I regretted my TV design rant last time I was in his store. I actually knew, even before he got to the point, why I was here -- the purpose of Pacita's presence. I knew that she was there to somehow act as a counter-balance to my thoughts. I watched as Eric almost wheeled her forward like a prize trophy. He was sweating and getting excited. I looked closely at his polyester shirt, by the armpit, and I convinced myself that I could see the wet odour patches spreading like an ink leak.

"Pacita this is Adrian Adrian this is Pacita."

"Hello", I replied.

"Pacita's a lecturer at Edinburgh. She is married to my cousin Lucas – you know Lucas?"

"You know I don't."

"Last time you were in my shop you had my head in a spin, saying that we're stuck with a miserable TV design."

"You shouldn't take me too seriously."

"You made me feel a little depressed. TVs are my business."

"I wasn't attacking you as a trader."

Eric ignored my efforts to play down the situation.

"Pacita, tell him about your project."

Pacita spoke on request about her Human Techno-Reactional Evolution (HTRE) theory. She said it was the future and that there were lots of ideas that we could adopt to complement technology, but the technology we have deserves better. She said technology needed us to develop as a species before we could make any real advancements.

I looked at her sceptically, as she continued to tell me that we could come up with new designs, but that they would be limited advancements, whereas HTRE will be a real new age, making technology less dangerous to us, so that we can fully interact with it.

"So, human evolution will help us totally change the designs of fridges and televisions?" I asked.

"We as a species, evolving, will be the ultimate design technology is craving. There's no point improving inanimate objects. Human evolution is imminent, a sophisticated change will happen, which will give us new potential, no longer will we need to solely relying on appliances."

"Really", I said. I was partly being sarcastic, but another part of me was intrigued. Pacita expanded on her theory, stating that researchers were already experimenting with microphones embedded in tooth fillings that link to an ear-piece, to replace the mobile phone. But she cautioned that this wasn't a pure HTRE initiative. HTRE was about the actual human body changing. For example subtle changes in the size of pupils, as the iris muscles start to contract pupils more than they dilate them. Pacita said this will be a result of the 24-hour television and monitor age allowing more light, at close range, to constantly pass through our eyes. The pupil won't need to expand as much as it does now as our time in darkness is reduced.

8

THE TABLES WERE dressed to precision. Star-like flashes shone from the rims of the wine glasses. Precision and shine symbolised the restaurant's quality. The waiter took Avril's shawl and coat and looked at me oddly for having braved the cold New Year's Eve night without the lightest of jackets. We sat down and tried to identify the people in the pictures on the walls. The waiter returned and took it upon himself to help us out. He pointed out three portraits of Thomas Wolsey, Henry VIII and Thomas Cromwell that were hanging together on one part of the wall. He said the owner of the establishment believed that the three men collectively shaped the mercurial England that we see today: revolution, diplomacy and war were each doctrines championed by one or more of the three men. Another section of the wall was adorned with framed photos of The Beatles and there were Turner and Constable prints near the entrance. Having finished acting as our tour guide, the waiter was drawn to my footwear.

"Lovely pair of shoes you're wearing: nice black leather and socks."

"Is there a problem?" I asked examining the shoes for myself, after I realised the waiter had a nervous tone to his voice.

"Well our dress code does not permit this. You can wear shoes, but they have to be suede loafers and we do not allow socks. On this occasion, seeing as it's New Year's Eve and you're with such a lovely woman, we will let it pass."

He spoke with a smugness that suggested he had pulled off a great humanitarian act. Avril frowned and looked at the waiter as if he was teasing us.

"It all seems very continental if you ask me, but I thought the restaurant calls itself The Traditional – its slogan being: *A true English restaurant?*"

The waiter rolled his eyes and relaxed his posture as if he'd been asked that question a thousand times.

"Yes madam. But what's traditional? We can't pinpoint Englishness. There were the Romans, Saxons...you know. English has to be part of the greater tradition – Europe." I speculated that during the daytime the waiter was a history undergraduate.

"Wearing suede loafers without socks isn't a custom across Europe – it might be common among Mediterranean people, but not the majority." I replied.

"You need to talk to management about the finer details" the waiter snapped back, "Are you ready to order sir?"

Avril was upstairs in bed. I wanted to join her, but Al had appeared at my door shortly after we'd returned from The Traditional, wanting to share a quick drink with me before getting back to his parents for the stroke of midnight. He moved a tuft of hair to one side, and flicked fluff off the sofa with his bony finger before blowing lightly into the half-full can of beer. It was annoying me, I couldn't fully engage with the New Year's Eve variety show on the TV. I put the TV on mute and decided to persevere with a conversation that we'd abandoned 10 minutes before.

"You listening to me?" I asked. "She didn't look too good. She was talking about divorce. It was awkward on the bus. You got to talk to her."

"We've spoken, agreed to divorce."

I was taken aback. He spoke so nonchalantly and I didn't realise permanent separation was a realistic outcome.

"How do you feel about that?"

"Not sure. The right thing I guess."

"I thought you two were for life."

"I'm in court soon too."

"You couldn't reach a settlement with Kate?"

"No, this is about Project Utopia."

"I hope you suck every last penny from them."

"Let's change the subject."

"Sorry I know it must be upsetting."

"Project Utopia gave me some of the best days of my life."

"You're crazy."

"It's true."

"I thought that woman at your conference was the human embodiment of your cyber woman?"

"I got speaking to her and she didn't share the same political opinions as the woman online."

"There was no woman online, remember? Get a grip, it wasn't reality."

Al sighed. He picked up another beer from the floor, and he swore as he failed to open it properly – the cap broke and the beer dribbled out into his glass. I took the TV off mute and continued watching my show.

9

THE GREY PAINT coatings on the poles were flaking, revealing rust with insipid brown and dirty-yellow tints. The poles held up wooden planks that were the temporary platforms for the workers. The shopping village was taking shape, along with its special features − the glass footpaths. I watched as two trucks entered the building site. The long, slim trucks carried sheets of glass in steel frames. I guessed that the steel framing would be used for the installation, an attachment system for the footpaths to be put together like Lego. I was about to walk off when I saw Avril out the corner of my eye, wearing a yellow hard hat. I turned to walk to her, but Christian caught sight of me and came over. The hard hat looked peculiar on him and his perverse image was complete when I noticed that he was wearing protective goggles over his glasses.

"Adrian, I need you brainstorming, not here watching us. Go discover our next big project. It's a new year and we need new inspiration." Christian said.

"I'm observing around this area today and I thought I'd take a quick peek. What's this complex going to be called?"

Christian said the Mayor wanted it to be named after himself, something like 'The Mayor Greenwood Shopping Village and Glass Paths'.

"Personally I think if we're going down the eponymous route, it should be named after Avril, or even you. Don't think that I've forgotten your contribution." There was a hint of jest in his voice.

I was reminded of Erykah Badu's track *AD 2000*: 'buildings won't be named after me – I'll go down dilapidated, my name will be misstated'.

Walking the streets I thought about having an easel so that I could paint my observations – writing was becoming a bore. With a pallet full of little squirts of oil paints, I could create impressions of the city. I could hang the pieces in a gallery and let the design department take inspiration from art. Let them nibble on camembert and white stilton and drink red wine while they pondered my meaning. But the reality required me to take to the streets, to walk them, write down my observations.

10

I SAW SCREENS AND monitors as objects that distorted reality. They were often instruments playing mellifluous tunes that were different to the world's miscellaneous sounds – a cacophony with lyrics that don't quiet rhyme. But when I returned to the office early from my wanderings, Anton's computer screen discredited this view by presenting a very stark reality. I had an aversion to emails being inadvertently exposed on a computer screen in the owner's absence. I'd come into the office and noticed Anton's exposed PC. I went to minimise Anton's email inbox, when I realised that the conversation he was having with Christian was about me:

> Chris,
>
> We have to cut costs. Adrian must go.
> Your thoughts on this?
>
> Regards
>
> Anton

I looked around the open-plan office, suspicious of everyone.

Margaret came up to me saying I looked lost – a euphemism for 'what are you doing peeking at Anton's PC, invading his privacy?'

Margaret was Anton and Christian's assistant. I had to think quickly, to make a snap judgment about whether or not she knew about the plot to sack me. If she didn't, then she could be useful as she had access to their personal email inboxes. I took a punt on Margaret being ignorant about the plot, and I started spinning lies to stun her into helping me. I told her there were rumours of some dodgy dealings possibly involving Anton and Christian. I expanded by saying head office wanted me to monitor their actions independent of the IT team – who may have had implicated staff members – and I needed her to give me her password, as she had access to their emails. I said I knew it was a serious breach of their privacy but that this was an extraordinary situation. I finished by saying that if she really didn't believe me then she was welcome to contact the Mayor directly. Margaret looked at me with a raised eyebrow and a hapless smile, which told me that she felt trapped into helping me because we both knew it was very unlikely that she would be bold enough to contact the Mayor.

As the end of the working day approached, everyone said their goodbyes. I was left with a cleaner who idly vacuumed the grey office carpet. I typed in Margaret's password and selected Anton's inbox. The emails concerning my downfall were incessant. I was perplexed, as I hadn't seen it coming in any shape or form. The passion with which Anton and Christian wrote about the subject was shocking:

Anton,

Adrian's job title was conjured from a desire to convince ourselves that we had found a new job role – which was almost poetic (a man wanders the streets for us and all we ask is that he writes down his thoughts). He is simply a glorified researcher and, apart from the glass suspension footpaths, we have seen little of value in any of his other reports.

Chris

Chris,

It's partly our fault, we've created a monster, an expensive monster. It's agreed we tell the Mayor we've found an area where we can cut costs. We can inform Adrian of this as soon as we have notified the Mayor.

Anton

I wanted to find more information about the plot. I continued to go through Anton's deleted items, randomly double-clicking and opening emails. I caught a glimpse of a name while clicking out of

one particular email. I clicked back in. My hand was
clammy and I could not work out whether it was my
sweat or the ceiling light that made the mouse glisten.
I had seen the name, so I had to read the email:

Anton,

I'll bear that in mind for next time. I
hope you enjoy your day.

Regards

Avril X

It seemed like a professional email, probably Anton
advising Avril about how to do things better in the
future. As a formality I scrolled down:

Dear Avril,

You shouldn't have rushed off this
morning.

Anton X

I sat very still. The cleaner had emptied all the
waste paper bins and placed fresh plastic bin liners
inside them. She walked out the office door, spraying
air freshener. I watched as the wire from the vacuum
cleaner trailed slowly after her.

11

I WENT TO WORK the following day. The weather was brutal, the wind made me tighten my lips and squint my eyes. The collar on my coat and my scarf were flapping frantically. My hands had dry white patches on the knuckles, in stark contrast to the rest of my skin. I searched for a small tub of Johnson's lotion in my coat pocket, rubbed some of the cream on knuckles, as I walked up Holloway Road from Highbury and Islington. I admired St Mary Magdalene's Church, astonished at how smooth its surface always looked – impervious to weather and time. I passed an all-day breakfast cafe, vintage furniture and textile shops, a pub that had been converted from a theatre, the grand Odeon cinema and several European fruit and vegetable mini-markets. I reached Archway tube station and continued the climb towards Highgate. I didn't have my notepad, so I stored particular observations in my head, and then I erased them from my mind, realising that there wasn't a need to work so assiduously for Anton and Christian any more. Instead I decided to respond to the rumblings in my stomach and have lunch. I found The Golden Batter Shop, next to the Orange School for Boys. I took my chips from the shop and I leaned on the window next to the shop's entrance before using a miniature wooden fork to pick my chips. School had finished and I watched boys in orange blazers rush past me with open mouths into The Golden Batter Shop. My eyes followed a black boy who was tall and skinny with low cut hair to the sides and bushy on top. He walked like a string puppet – maybe because his adolescent mind hadn't become accustomed to his adult body. He spoke loudly and articulately to a friend. I was slouched against the shop's window as he walked by. He spat out chewing gum that landed by my feet. I looked at him. He looked back and confronted my disgusted glare.

"And what? And what?", he said, walking into the chip shop with a few other boys who laughed at his temerity and called his name, Dwaine. They told him to forget me and get some food. I stood my ground, stubborn, not willing to be moved along by juveniles. The boys ordered their food and came out of the shop chewing their chips furiously. Dwaine was walking slightly behind the group. He finally reached me and it seemed his conscience had reprimanded him.

"Listen, sorry yeah. I came on strong. But don't glare me yeah. I don't like that."

"I was glaring because you spat chewing gum by my feet, but apology accepted."

Dwaine's friends looked back to him and saw that he was in conversation with me. One boy was particularly annoyed by our more convivial-looking interaction. He told Dwaine to leave me – the old fool – alone. Dwaine cursed the friend, leaving him to retreat into his portion of chips. I smiled at Dwaine: I was warming to him. But I couldn't get the image of him spitting gum out of my head. It had instantly transformed the ground it had stuck to – depressing the concrete. My mind was hyper-active, I instantly thought how brutal a picture it would be for glass structures to be immersed in saliva-glazed chicle. I was feeling both liberated and a little crazy since reading the emails between Anton and Christian – a plan was developing in my head to exact revenge on Avril and my bosses. I was developing a plot. I needed impressionable minds and bold characters, like Dwaine. I acted decisively and asked Dwaine for his number, telling him that I might have some paid work for him and a few of his friends in the near future.

Later that night, I studied Al as he dropped ice into a glass and poured vodka in stages. He was trying to convince me that he was actually measuring the volume.

"You want some?"

"No, I'm good."

I observed Al a little longer – as carefully and quietly as I had done during our *Race for Marina* – trying to work him out.

"How do you find it? Do you feel different?", I enquired.

"How's what?"

"Cheating, being a cheat?"

"It wasn't cheating in the physical sense."

"You would have."

"True, but it didn't get to that stage, I don't know. Why the questioning, why wait all this time to ask? Is something happening with you? Are you cheating on Avril?"

"It's just a question", I said, feeling slightly exposed.

"Or is she cheating on you?"

"Drop it, you idiot!" I then took the bottle of vodka from Al and poured myself a large amount to drink.

12

I COULDN'T RECOGNISE A thing. Perplexed, I turned
back to page 332. No clues were there. I turned to
pages further back, searching for a line, a word, that was
familiar – anything to give me the security I needed to
believe that I was understanding the text. I hit a name I
remembered on page 282. I started reading again from
there – apprehensive that it wouldn't be any use and
I still wouldn't be able to fully comprehend the plot.
I slammed the book shut at page 290 and flipped my
head back, my eyes facing the ceiling. Avril was in the
kitchen cooking, it was my kitchen – the least she could
do was feed me. I wondered whether the dish she was
preparing was similar to one she'd cooked for Anton.
Avril brought over the food; her black and brown hair
extensions were in a ponytail, the sleeves on blouse
were pushed up on her arms to her biceps. After dinner
I tried hard to openly show that I was angry at her – I
gave her one-word answers, gazed into nowhere when
she spoke and turned the television volume up high.
She didn't seem to be disturbed by my behaviour. I
took that to mean I was now insignificant. Now that

Anton was on the scene, Avril was just going through the motions with me.

The next day shot forward at a great velocity. Before I knew it, I'd finished taking notes for the day and I was back at the office. The office was nearly empty. A printer was churning out a load of paper, producing a sweeping sound as the printed sheets emerged onto the tray. I looked at the general stillness of the office. It symbolised what I found inviting about the job. After a full day walking the streets of London, my bosses and most of the workforce were leaving – I had no real contact with them. I snapped out of my thoughts when Dietmar approached. He usually worked late and we'd become friends because he was often still in the office when I got back. I liked the consistency of his presence, and the good company. We would sometimes arrange to meet up outside of work but he would never show, always making some excuse. He was right to stand me up: our relationship was solely about two men who united in order to get through the working day. There was only one aim for the relationship: one reason for its existence.

"Have you read this?", he asked, as he held up the front page of his broadsheet.

"I was reading about it this morning?"

"Looks like we're heading to war." Dietmar continued.

"I think we'll stick with the UN, they didn't approve the resolution amendment."

"You don't see the way our man fawns over Bush?"

I smiled at Dietmar. Our late afternoon conversations didn't usually feature politics. Usually it was football or a colleague who was annoying us.

13

THE REPORT WAS a detailed description of a plot to lace the suspended glass footpaths with gum: chewing gum, bubble gum and other types of sticky confectionery. The idea had come to me outside The Golden Batter Shop. Dwaine spitting out chewing gum was a powerful and vulgar act. The concrete slab that it had landed on was new, it hadn't been absorbed properly by its surrounding slabs but the chicle still managed to make it look worn and dated. Dwaine's act had captured my imagination. My plot was a desperate act to buy time before I was sacked – it would give me a few months to sort myself out, to make money and relocate. The obvious target had to be the footpaths: it was a way of netting all three deceivers. I worked hard into the night. The muffled sounds of the flat's mechanisms – the pipes, the ignition of the boiler, the soft vibration of the fridge – gave me a calm demeanour while I created the pseudo report. The next day, after I'd made my morning observations, Christian called me in to discuss the paper that I'd left on his desk. I entered the office. He raised his hand, motioning for me to take the seat opposite him. Anton joined us, taking a seat next to Christian. They looked very similar in appearance: they both had short brown hair and wore V-neck sweaters between a shirt and a blazer. The only significant variable was their glasses. Christian wore thick luminous-blue frames, while Anton had clear glasses with lenses that dominated an ultra-thin frame.

"I had the Mayor on the phone. He's taking this seriously", Christian said.

Anton removed his glasses and picked up his copy of the report, bringing it close to his face to see it clearly.

"The report says you heard kids talking. It could be just that: talk", Anton said.

I picked up my copy of the report and flicked to page 5. I knew it intimately: I was prepared.

"My report refers to previous observations that I've made."

"Go on?", Christian guided.

"I've previously observed outbreaks of this new type of graffiti. It definitely exists."

"Where?"

"Hoxton, Camden, Brixton …"

"So spray paint is out, and gum's in?" Christian joked.

"Kids call it 3D graffiti."

"You're sure the kids you heard talking aren't actually involved?"

"Yes, I didn't get that impression. I took their contact details, saying that I might have work for a couple of them. I was thinking ahead, in case we needed more information from them."

"The target is definitely the shopping village?",
Anton asked as he read on.

"I heard they think attacking the glass footpaths
will have a big impact."

"I fear there's an air of paranoia in all of this."
Anton suggested.

"Paranoia doesn't exist in this century. Nothing
can be classed as hyperbole, the truth of an event out
runs its own speculation these days."

"You're suggesting that Camden should be on
lockdown?"

"I do."

I stared solidly at Anton, to reinforce my sincere
persona. He was staring back, wanting to find cracks
in my demeanour, but he eventually resigned himself
to the fact that he couldn't.

"Surprisingly, as I said, the Mayor's taking this
seriously", Christian continued.

"Good, I don't think it can be ignored."

"The footpaths are supposed to be part of his
legacy."

I relaxed and took a sip of water from the glass in
front of me.

"We've been instructed by the Mayor to second
you to a position where you will lead on preventing
this alleged sabotage. It'll be exactly how you
recommended in the report." Christian said.

Anton tossed the report across the table and put
his glasses back on. He'd seemed the more sceptical of
the two.

"We were thinking about making changes to your
role anyway, but we can talk more about that after
your secondment", he said with a smile.

I stared at Anton, until he moved his gaze from me. I wanted to throw my water over him, to slide across the table and hit him. Instead I got up and gave reassurances to my bosses that my mission would be successful. I then left the office.

GUM GRAFFITI

14

A 'BAN FRENZY' PROLIFERATED the globe early in the 21st century. Swearing was banned in the Mexican city of Zapopan. The city of Geneva banned beef from school canteens – during the 'mad cow' episode. In Sao Paulo and Rio de Janeiro, circuses and shows consisting of performing animals were prohibited. Chewing gum was banned from the Camden borough of London by the Mayor; the resulting tabloid puns were painfully bad but paradoxically true of public opinion: 'It's begumming a joke' and 'Gum on, you can't be serious!', were a few that I can recall. The Mayor worked strenuously to defend his decision to ban chicle. He assured people that it was only until he'd foiled a plot to destroy one of north London's most innovative developments. He appeared on live local TV, intransigent as the audience jibed and booed. Mayor Greenwood countered the diatribes by talking passionately about our way of life being threatened by a new age of terrorism where, and I quote 'the blunt can be made sharp'. He was also convinced that building the shopping village, with its unique paths, would guarantee his election as Mayor for another term. He bought into the notion that light-reflecting footpaths, however small their scale, would help to reduce crime. His morale was further boosted by a letter from the President of Singapore – an extract from the letter read:

> *Singapore is proud to call the Mayor of London a partner in the global struggle against antisocial behaviour. We would, however, like the Mayor to commit to making the chewing gum ban London wide, and not just restricted to Camden. We also would like the ban to remain in place after the threat to the footpaths has subsided. As we have banned gum since 1992, we are more than happy to send a delegation to London to teach you the techniques that we have used to stop gum being smuggled in from Malaysia. The challenge for you is somewhat greater, as the pressure on Camden from the rest of the capital could mean that greater resources are needed to counter the gum threat. We challenge you to go further and to look into issues such as banning spitting and banning people from leaving public toilets unflushed after urinating ...*

Camden Council ordered gum repossession vans to visit newsagents, mini-markets, nightclubs, schools, pubs and newspaper stands to collect all chewing gum. The Council argued that the repossessions were a convenient service for local businesses – ensuring a stress-free clear out of the product. A stop and search policy was in force for people entering the Camden borough. The management of the London Underground was ordered to stop using gum-smelling liquid to clean the ground in order to mask the smell of sick, alcohol and urine. Dried pieces of chicle on concrete paving stones were removed by high-pressure water nozzles, dry ice and lasers, so that the authorities could monitor new outbreaks that were likely to appear as a result of black market sales.

The black market was on the agenda for the operation team that I had formed, called FOGY (Fighting Off Gum Youth). The team members were Justin Peacock, Ian Locke and Mathew Headman. Our headquarters was a run-down confectionery factory that was located in Camden, between Hampstead Road and Euston station. The factory had been re-painted and the majority of the machinery had been removed. We sat around a glass meeting table, on black leather chairs – sparing no expense with the Mayor's funds.

"Firstly, everyone needs to know the history of Al Capone." I said.

"Why?" Justin asked.

He played with his dark-ginger hair and mimicked adjusting the fat knot in his black and blue striped tie, by holding the knot and moving his hand left to right with little actual movement. It seemed to be a nervous fidget. Justin, like the others, was a fresh university graduate who longed for a career in the civil service. When he'd been given the job profile for the FOGY assignment by the Employment Agency, he'd thought it would look good on his CV when he eventually applied for work with the Foreign Office as a desk clerk in some remote British Embassy.

"Al Capone was the quintessential bootlegger – I want everyone here to understand his mindset."

"I still don't get the connection?" Justin pressed.

"Banning gum will inevitably create bootleggers." I replied, irritated.

Justin flipped back the cover of his silver laptop. The tapping of his typing resounded around the hollow factory as he searched the internet.

"OK, I've got some facts."

"Great."

He continued to say that prior to 1919 Capone was arrested for minor offences. Then he went into partnership with John Torrio. They ran a bootlegging business together. Capone later inherited the business, became very successful and his crimes couldn't be pinned on him for some time. I stood up for dramatic effect, pointing my finger in front of me as I spoke.

"I'm looking to pin down every kid who tries to sabotage the footpath project. Gum, their weapon of choice, cannot be available underground. It's our job to make sure this is the case."

The three men nodded, indicating that they were ready for the challenge. We all then went for a late breakfast, before I told them to go home to prepare for the task ahead and to come back tomorrow to start in earnest.

That afternoon, with the FOGY team gone, three adolescent boys – Dwaine Dube, Farooq Uddin and Tray Trae – entered the factory for their briefing. I devised another acronym for this group, GTC (Gum The City). I had called Dwaine a few days before, reminding him of our encounter at the chip shop. I asked if he was interested in paid work that wasn't entirely above board and whether he had a couple of friends, that he could trust, who could join him.

"Are you guys really chewing gum? These meetings need you to be punctual and you're an hour late!", I said.

"We want to talk cash first", said Dwaine. Then he rapped: "*We might be sixteen / but it's the green / that first must be seen / If you know what I mean / it's a big price you pay for hiring the A team*".

Tray laughed. He was shorter than Dwaine, black and muscular with limp strands of hair on his chin, which made him look untidy rather than older.

"*I wanna be big earning / swim in a pool of sterling / want excess that I can be burning / I wanna buy a Lex and get heads turning*", Tray added.

Farooq was the quiet one. He had a full beard and, in certain lights, looked like a man. He simply smiled at his friends' cockiness.

"Very nice boys, very lyrical", I said.

"Yeah, who said poetry's dead, it has just evolved", Dwaine replied.

I was impressed by how business-orientated the boys were. The terms and conditions had to be right. They weren't allowing me to dictate the crucial subject of payment. I had to compromise. I told them I'd give them each 500 now and if the operation succeeded, I'd transfer the rest from wherever I was in the world after the operation. They begrudgingly agreed before Farooq realised he'd better ask what they were getting themselves in to. Duplicity and sabotage was my response. I informed the boys that they would be involved in countering the efforts of Camden Council's FOGY task force. Redistributing seized gum. The logic in redistribution would be to convince my employers that black market gum activity was widespread, making them more receptive to my demands for more surveillance equipment to help suppress the black market. I explained to the boys that the surveillance equipment would be sold and I would share the proceeds of sale with them. As well as raising funds for our future, I also told them the other task would be sabotaging the glass footpaths, in the new Camden shopping village, with gum graffiti.

I felt like a criminal mastermind. Then suddenly I had palpitations as I realised, right then, that I'd crossed the line. I was a gangster, a fraudster – I'd be another shameful black statistic behind bars.

"Why you doing all this?", Tray asked.

"Revenge, money and pride", I stated.

I almost hugged Tray for bringing me out of my fear trance, for helping me to focus and reminding me what my plan was all about.

Just before closing time, I was in Eric's shop. He punched in a code to open the door to his storeroom. The room was dim, it had a stale smell and a leak from a crack in the ceiling. We turned left, away from the stacked goods and I was puzzled as to why the storeroom seemed so expansive, larger than the actual shop floor. Eric opened a door, which squeaked and hung loosely from its hinges. Inside was a small office. It was littered with paper – invoices, sheets of perforated price stickers and handwritten notes. He sat down at his computer, manoeuvred the mouse, double-clicked, and then finally the unhealthy sound of a dated printer was heard. I turned to the printer and a single sheet of paper emerged. Eric handed it to me. It was the email from Juan Carlos Lopez – the El Salvadorian.

"Here take it. It has his email address on the top of the page. What you want it for anyway?"

"Mr Lopez is in the market for some intelligence equipment and I've got my hands on some products that might interest him", I replied.

"What kinda friend are you? Here I am, your Greek pal, and you want to sell to an El Salvadorian?"

Eric said half joking and half serious.

"Let's just say they're not the type of products that you want to be caught with."

"I never knew you were a dealer. You handling *hot* goods?", Eric asked.

"Stuff I acquired through work."

"You stealing from the London Assembly?"

"Put it this way: I've checked surveillance items out, but I won't be checking them back in."

Eric shook his head in disbelief and escorted me back out to the shop floor.

15

IMPOUNDED CHICLE WAS taken to the factory by the FOGY task force. All chicle was processed – boxed, labelled and dated. Even a single stick or tablet of gum was filed in this way. The day had been very productive in terms of seizing the black-market goods, so I rewarded the task force with the afternoon off. When they'd left, I called the GTC team to the factory. They arrived and I handed them gum, which they put in backpacks. They shot off on mountain bikes and left the gum on street corners, in industrial mobile bins, at Camden Lock Market, at the foot of tower blocks and in Regent's Park – just off the beaten tracks, in high grass. They watched the clients that they'd coerced (by cold calling or chance meetings) collect the chicle from these pre-agreed locations. This had been regular activity for several weeks. The GTC would sell black market gum to corrupt sweet shop owners, the weak, the greedy, the liberal occupants of cheap Camden rentals and nightclub owners – who, in turn, peddled gum they received to customers against a backdrop of flashing lights and pumping beats.

When a deal was on the verge of going through, they passed word to me and I informed the FOGY team, who I'd strategically placed near the transaction sites. I told them that my informers had tipped me off about the black market deals. Justin, Mathew and Ian jumped at the chance of raiding perpetrators. To them it was preparation for their ultimate goal of working for MI5 or MI6 after building experience in the foreign office. I doubted their chances, as they didn't even have the sense to audit the gum that was coming into the factory – they foolishly believed that they were making progress on removing all gum from Camden. I felt guilty for entrapping the public by selling them black market gum that I had banned in the first place. But if I didn't put the gum back out there, my FOGY task force would have been deemed a success and it would have been closed down. I wouldn't have been able to press for more expensive equipment to tackle the black market dealers. The equipment was to be my meal ticket; this operation was to be my revenge.

We met a month after Camden had introduced chicle restrictions. We sat at the corner of a glass table, leaning on it, making the meeting more personal. We spoke in whispers, as if we were being watched. Anton removed his designer glasses and placed them on the glass table, where the two items almost merged into one entity. His eyes looked like they were struggling to open. Maybe he needed to keep wearing his glasses but he wanted to show the seriousness of what he was about to say by taking them off. He asked me why I was spending tens of thousands on top-end surveillance equipment. Anton said he and the Mayor were concerned. He reminded me that security cameras had been set up around the shopping village site. Everything was secure. My FOGY task force had their own laptops and phones along with support from Camden repossession teams. I had to forcefully portray an image of a morbid situation that we were facing, in order to defend my spending.

"We're in an age where consumer products are the weapons of new-age terrorists and anti-social perpetrators. We're in an age where the blunt is made sharp. There should be no questioning of my methods or how much I spend to protect our way of life."

Anton looked at me as if I'd taken leave of my senses.

"Half the stuff on these invoices are not in use. Justin and the others say they didn't know such equipment was being purchased. Where are the goods?"

"I've stored them away until they're needed", I said.

"So you're using our budget to buy things for situations that may or may not arise?" Anton said, pulling at his V-neck jumper.

"Anticipation."

"Don't get smart— I'm still your boss. Chris and I recommended you to Greenwood because you have informers. I'm watching you very closely."

I enjoyed irritating the man sleeping with my girlfriend.

"Those kids, do they know about the FOGY team?"

"No. The kids are totally in the dark."

My face was like stone, not giving anything away.

"Good. I don't want those kids to know about FOGY. They could be two-way informers".

That afternoon, the boys came to the factory after truanting from school while working for me. They hung their orange blazers on the back of the leather chairs. Tray had the end of his tie cut short, diagonally, an anti-establishment fashion statement. He began swinging in his chair: it was squeaking, which annoyed me.

"Cut it out!"

"What's up with you? My man needs to chill – getting all angry and shit!"

The veins in his gym-enhanced neck throbbed.

"Fresh from school and talking weirdly again. What is 'my man'? I'm not your man!", I replied, not able to contain my wonder at their use of language. Dwaine responded as if he'd anticipated that today I would question the way they spoke.

"It's intelligent talk you know. Ask the great linguistic thinkers, like William Labov. 'Treat language descriptively instead of prescriptively' – I learnt that reading at home. I'm reading a lot these days, so much now I'm reading. So don't judge. Don't slam my slang."

Dwaine grinned to reveal two rows of well-set teeth. His sharpness impressed me: I'd been fascinated by the boy ever since our first encounter. I told him he was a joy to know. So confident, so cool and precocious. I teased Tray and Farooq, asking why some of Dwaine's intellect and coolness hadn't rubbed-off on to them. Tray perked up.

"He ain't cool. He's getting weird. What's 'so much now I'm reading'? Who talks like that?!"

Tray had a point. Although Dwaine was usually clever with language, it was never pretentious. I looked over to him and noticed that he was using face wipes, rigorously scrubbing his hands.

"Are you alright Dwaine?" I said, becoming disturbed by his actions.

"The air's poisonous and dust mites are everywhere."

"He's been talking like this all day" Farooq said.

I wondered whether the pressure of the operation was taking its toll on Dwaine, whether he'd suddenly realised the magnitude of the consequences.

"If you're not feeling too well, go home for the day. We can cope without you."

Dwaine ignored me and continued to scrub his hands, repeatedly muttering about poisonous air and dust mites. I thought that if I could get him to look at me, straight in the eyes, I could cure whatever infliction had infiltrated him. I touched his shoulder. He shrugged me off and ran to the door, shouting about the dust mites.

"Shouldn't someone go after him, see if he's alright?"

"Don't watch that, watch me. This is a *long ting*. We've been giving gum to people for time and you still can't pay us more than that £500 you gave us on the first day?", Farooq said, springing into life. He looked younger with his beard shaved, although he had dark, sleep-deprived skin under his eyes. I repeated my plan to sell the surveillance gear at the end of the operation and share the funds with the team. I then asked Farooq and Tray to go after their troubled friend.

It was late. I knocked on the door of Al's parents' house, angry that he'd made me drive there. I'd had a long day and I wasn't sure that I had the strength to deal with quirky Al. His mum answered the door; she had perfected the fake smile and she looked beyond me to see whether I was alone. She'd known me since I was a child but didn't trust anyone who wasn't family. I went into Al's bedroom. He was on his knees with his back to me, searching excitedly in the lower part of his wardrobe. He spoke to me without turning around.

"I'm sure I have some hardcopies in my suitcase."

"Of what?", I replied, looking around his bedroom, admiring the exactness and timelessness of the room. It hadn't changed since we were kids. On the wall there was a heavy gold frame with a photo of Marina inside. I smiled, as I was sure this was his way of keeping ahead in the *Race for Marina*.

"The conversations: the emails from Project Utopia – the girl. Helena."

"Helena. She has a name!", I retorted.

He intensified his search and emerged victorious.

"Got them!"

"What do you want them for? Don't tell me you want to frame them, encase them in glass and then hang them on your wall next to Marina."

"My solicitor needs them. Needs evidence to show the full scale of the deceit."

Al handed me the emails. His hair was messy, bland and dirty looking, with new grey strands standing up. His green and grey eyes were wide open, crazed. I feared I was losing my best friend.

16

HIS BEARD WAS white with black undertones, resting on slightly wrinkled black skin. He wore a faded 'Free Mandela' sweater, a beanie hat and dark-blue cords. I stopped arguing about payment with Farooq and Tray when I noticed him standing there. I took careful backward steps to one of the damp factory walls. I wasn't sure whether the man was an agent of the Mayor's, a Camden resident looking for gum or some random oddball who'd stumbled on factory and wanted a chat.

"Don't be alarmed."

"You shouldn't be here."

"I'm Dwaine Dube."

"Is this a joke?"

"The senior. The Dwaine you know is my son."

"Who says I know your son?"

"You do."

I looked at Tray and Farooq for confirmation that this was their friend's father. Their expressions didn't contradict the man, but in typical teenage fashion they didn't enthusiastically endorse him.

"Where's Dwaine, your son?"

"Hikikomori."

"I don't understand?"

I was getting more impatient than nervous: the man wasn't getting to his purpose quickly enough. Then he finally told me that hikikomori was a prevalent condition in Japan that mainly affected teenage boys. Something sets a trigger off in them, and they lock themselves in a room and remain there indefinitely. They eat, defecate, and conduct their whole life in a bedroom or kitchen. Dwaine senior said that his son was the first person to be diagnosed with hikikomori outside of Japan. I moved from the damp wall towards Dwaine senior.

"I'm sorry to hear about your son. Last time I saw him he was acting a bit strangely, but I didn't know about the hikikomori."

"No one could have predicted it."

"He was working for me part time after school, with these two – advising on teenager culture. I wasn't honest at first because it's secret work. I work for the Mayor. Can I ask why you've come?"

"I know what you're doing, what my son was doing" Dwaine senior said. He didn't have an angry or accusative tone. He made his statement only as a matter of fact.

"He told you?"

Dwaine senior said he spoke to his son through his bedroom door. He wanted his father to replace him on the GTC team.

I was receiving a tsunami of information; I needed to create a canal in my mind so that I could control the flow.

"You really know what we're planning, what we want to do?", I asked. Dwaine senior replied by saying he knew exactly what he was getting involved in and if it helped him remain close to his son and keep the dialogue open, then he'd do anything. I relied on my intuition: he seemed trustworthy and he seemed bound to us by the commitment that he had made to his son. I asked him what he could offer us as a team.

"In my teens I was a member of the uMkhonto we Sizwe. I didn't actually bomb bridges or buildings but I arranged transportation and other necessities needed to carry out our forceful politics."

"Terror", I said hesitantly.

"Knowledge of what it takes to carry out strategic operations, which I believe this GTC team is all about."

I was relieved that he was bizarrely sympathetic to my cause – be it genuine or for the sake of his son. We shook hands and I started to brief him in more detail about my girlfriend, my employers and the gum operation. It felt peculiar knowing that another adult would be involved in the gum plot. I thought what I was doing was childish – vandalising a bridge – but then Dwaine senior seemed to be secure with the idea, serious and not mocking. He strengthened the legitimacy of the operation. It was easy to persuade impressionable kids but Dwaine senior was a grown man.

Avril knew something was wrong but she said nothing. She gazed at the TV. The thumbnail on her right hand was picking a fingernail on left hand. Her upper lip slid along her lower lip, playing with applied lip balm. I had the remote control for the video player in my hand. I rewound the tape with the visuals still showing. A figure walked backwards, quickly and comically, behind a thick black line that crossed the front of the screen. I pressed play and there, in Technicolor, was Louis Jourdan singing in the film Gigi. He sang about Gigi in a condescending way, then affectionately, then condescendingly, then affectionately. The song finished. I rewound it again, turning my face, but not my gaze, in Avril's direction.

"I love this song, this film. See how Gigi works him into a frenzy?"

Avril looked at me, puzzled.

"Are you okay?"

"Yes." I said, with contempt.

In the morning I contacted both gum teams. They seemed organised, knew what they had to do for the day, so I paid a visit to the Design and Development Agency. I wanted to catch the office off guard, to get a sense of the office's vibe and see whether word had spread about my downfall. I said that the purpose of my visit was to finish off a few reports that I'd been working on before I was seconded to deal with the gum plot. There were no lingering looks when I got there, no air of awkwardness, but then again I couldn't be sure. I went over to Dietmar. He moved the mouse with quick, gentle touches. I looked at his monitor to see what the mouse translated to the screen. Dietmar looked up at me.

"Oh, it's you. What brings the Mayor's right-hand man down here?"

"Thought I'd check up on you guys."

"We should feel privileged."

"And of course there's the paper work."

"Of course."

"How've you been, what's the gossip?" I said, watching his movements, looking for any sudden change – wanting to know if he knew about me.

"I've been fine. Gossip? No time to gossip."

"There's always time for gossip."

"Never mind that. Pass me that printout over there. Bloody paper backups. Computers are still not trusted here. We can save files to CDs and to different drives but they still want paper files. They're turning computers into metal carts, and we are the horses doing the pulling", Dietmar complained.

Margaret had been watching me from the moment I entered the office. I greeted a few people who congratulated me for safeguarding Avril's project, before I finally made my way towards Margaret. She looked at me as if I was her husband returning from a hunt, waiting to see whether I had brought back food for the family.

"Margaret, how are you?"

"They're still here. I trust you want more access?"

"Access?"

"Anton and Christian. The investigation?"

"Oh yes" I said, searching my mind for a convincing story that I could use to explain how things had developed. I was still puzzled about why Margaret was excitingly badgering me. She had passwords, she could have looked at Anton's and

Christian's emails and put two and two together. Maybe she knew that it was all lies but she was a fully signed up fantasist who thrived on my fiction.

"So what's going on?"

"We investigated and we found nothing" I said. "Routine kind of thing."

Peculiarly, I was pleased. Although I knew I was on the verge of being sacked, I hadn't been handed complete indignity. From what I could see, my colleagues had no knowledge that the high status that I had acquired was on brittle legs. The fear I had was similar to Kate's. It was one thing being betrayed but what was worse was betrayal being common knowledge, denting the pride further. I understood now why she desperately called me that night to find out if I knew about Al's cyber affair.

17

M Y FINGERS WERE cold, tingling with a
sensation like pins and needles. It was a Sunday
and the four of us stood with the police watching
the crowds gathered in Camden's Stables Market.
Justin was in a three-quarter length coat. He had a
notepad and a pen in his hand, ready to make notes
if needed. He regularly and coarsely scratched his
ginger stubble as he studied the crowd. Mathew
looked sternly ahead, trying to keep warm in his pea
coat by stamping on the spot. He was balding but he
didn't wear a hat – his skin was peeling on the bald
patches. Ian's head was insulated by thick side-burns
and his long brown hair. He wore a black roll neck,
jeans and trainers. He was the one who couldn't keep
a straight face. He was turning around constantly
to look at the police officers, wanting them to share
his incredulity at the naked protesters on the streets
who were holding banners that issued commands
such as 'THE MAYOR'S DUMB. GIVE US BACK
GUM' and 'GIVE US GUM OR WE'LL REMAIN
NAKED AND NUMB'. The protest coincided with

the arrival of the Singapore delegation, who had come to Camden to visit the Mayor and share their ideas and experiences in dealing with chicle in a banned environment. The trench coats, scarves, beanie hats, jeans, jumpers and shoes that the protesters had arrived in rested peacefully on the ground. We were there in our FOGY team capacity to see whether we could seek out the ringleaders: those who might have acted as bootleggers at night.

As the sun set and the majority of protesters started to reach for their belongings, the police scaled down their horseback officers and the TV satellite vans withdrew, having captured enough footage, a nucleus of die-hard protesters remained. Some of them chewed gum and were dragged away by the police. Some jumped up and down vigorously, shouting and shaking banners, and others sat still on the steps shivering in the cold – they were the true naturists. My eyes caught sight of a lady who was not naked. She was fully clothed. My eyes focused and I saw that it was Pacita De La Cruz. Her black hair was cut to shoulder length and she wore pink earmuffs and pink gloves. She was holding a sign that read 'GUM FOR EVOLUTION'. I walked over to where she was standing.

"What are you doing here?" I said, with clear disappointment in my voice.

"Banning gum could hinder HTRE. You know my line of work" Pacita said, struggling to raise her voice above the chanting of the remaining crowd.

"You're acting like a mad bohemian professor."

"I'm not a professor."

"Lecturer, professor, whatever you do at Edinburgh University."

"I teach children at a primary school in Edinburgh. Eric was misleading when he introduced me. Apart from introducing my students to HTRE during a science month, this project is my own."

"I don't get why you're here?"

"Our teeth?"

"Teeth now, not eyes." I said sardonically.

Pacita acted as if she couldn't detect my ridicule. She calmly explained that teeth wouldn't be left behind in the evolution. She believed that technology – including microwaves, cookers and blenders – generally softened food. Teeth no longer needed to work as hard, and some people are now fed intravenously. She said that HTRE will see teeth reduce in size and become lighter and blunt – easier to break.

I responded by asking why this would be good for us, why we needed weaker teeth. Conversely adverts are always convincing us that chewing gum strengthens teeth – so to support her theory she should delight in the chicle ban.

Pacita gently pushed away a bare hip that came in close proximity to her. She then returned to my challenge. She said that she believed chewing gum would have little impact on strengthening teeth as our bodies adapt to the fact that our diets increasingly involve softer food. She said that she couldn't explain why weaker teeth will be of benefit, but that somehow it would be linked to advancement – it would help us to interact better with technology. Therefore she was against any ban on soft food, as it would slow down the process of human evolution. After Pacita had finished speaking, I ordered two police officers to escort away what I was convinced was a confused, eccentric woman.

The GTC team were in the factory after I returned there alone from the protest. They were drawing on giant corrugated plastic sheets, carving out letter shapes with sharp blades, thinking up new words or new 'tags', as the graffiti experts would say. We'd entered the next stage of the operation: with the opening of the shopping village approaching, it was time to prepare the sabotage campaign. I supervised the stencil-making efforts from a chair in the corner of the room. Now and again I popped my head up, complimenting the various stencils that the team had created. The rest of the time, I had my head in my book. I'd read 547 pages. Dwaine senior looked over to me.

"Good book?"

"It's getting better."

"What genre?"

"Fiction."

"Fiction. Why don't you read some real literature? Not the fake but the real, the past. My land for example, my peoples' struggles."

As he spoke, I was aware of the strained look on his face that I hadn't noticed before. He looked like a man who had been battling all his life.

"That's a heavy subject."

"I have a good book about South Africa in the 20th century."

"I know about Apartheid, the African National Congress, Nelson and Winnie, the Youth League, the Boer War, Rhodes, the Rivonia trial ..."

"You're just reeling off words and names. You're not showing me that you know."

"What do I need to know?"

"About black people being put in mining compounds, given electric shocks and kept for slave labour."

"I know this."

"The unjustified detainings and killings. Everyday life for blacks – that's what you need to know, what you need to read about." Dwaine senior spoke with passion, but I continued to read my book, defiant in the face of fierce opposition.

18

Observation: unclassified 1

Camden still has a relationship with chicle. A grimy relationship, where Camden harbours chicle in obscure places. Out of sight: away from prying eyes. Chewed in alleys and basements. With all the efforts to eradicate it, still it's stuck in those historically referenced places — under desks and chairs, and on pavements.

I WAS NOW MAKING notes for myself instead of for City Hall. I wanted to record the impact of my actions. Maybe for my memoirs or maybe because I thought that I had a skill that needed to be exercised, regardless of whether or not I was receiving remuneration.

Later that evening Avril and I returned to the Traditional restaurant, in the correct attire. While our first visit had confused us, it had also made us curious. I adhered to the 'shoes *sans* socks' policy, having invested in a pair of Italian loafers from Camden Market. The weather that evening had been drizzly and I could feel water between my toes, trapped under the soles. I heard the squelch as the water was squashed between my feet and suede. We ate fried plantain and black-eyed pea stew for a starter. Avril had jollof rice and fried fish for her main dish, I ate ground rice and a pepper and onion stew with my fingers. Avril again questioned the waiter, asking why we were offered a non-English menu in what we believed was a traditional English restaurant. The waiter looked confused and laughed in response before delicately moving away to assist a couple on another table.

"You look good in the shirt and those loafers!" she said to me, as she cutely removed a small fish bone from between her glossy lips.

"You think?" I said, trying to be calm as piping hot ground rice tormented my fingertips.

"Absolutely!"

Her flattery invited me to soften up. Maybe I just needed to talk to her, to encourage her to tell me the truth. Maybe her honesty would stop my mad attack on her glass footpaths.

"We haven't really talked relationship, its trajectory", I said.

"We're doing good aren't we?"

"You happy, happy with me?", I asked.

I was probing, giving Avril a chance to cleanse her conscience.

"Actually no. It's over!"

My fingers dropped ground rice I'd moulded into a ball back into the bowl, causing the soup to splash. I looked at her with utter disgust.

"You're a disgrace!"

"Cool it. I'm kidding, what's wrong with you?" she replied, nervously looking around to see who'd heard the outburst.

"What?"

"I was teasing, you can't even see that. You seem to be off with me lately. I sense it, I know it. Have I done something wrong?"

"Nothing, let's just eat."

I didn't like this me – the moody beast – but it was necessary, she was hurting me. Avril didn't like my growing moods either. She told me that this couldn't go on. Her project, the shopping village, was launching in a couple of weeks. I was causing her anxiety. She said our relationship should be put on 'ice' until we had space to talk after the footpaths launched. I looked deep into her eyes, those poker eyes, they didn't betray her. If I didn't know better, I would've been convinced that I was breaking her heart.

"You're right Avril, I'm going to be busy myself, busy protecting your project. So on ice, as you say."

Avril looked at me dejected, seemingly upset at how easily I had agreed with her idea. Briefly, I felt like the wrong-doer, the one out of line. Then I felt enraged because that was what she wanted. She wanted me to doubt myself, to doubt what I knew.

I stopped at a supermarket after the silent drive to Avril's apartment, where I'd dropped her off. I bought a family packet of crisps and a pack of four beers. At the store exit, I turned back to look at the kiosk. People were buying photos of their visit to the store. A couple kissed each other after they saw the photo of themselves by isle thirteen. A family of five looked up at the monitor, pondering which of the four pictures on show they would buy. The youngest child excitedly jumped up in the air and pointed to the second photo, which showed the family picking apples in the fruit and vegetable section. At home I watched TV while drinking one of the beers, eating some *waakye* and fried fish. The London regional channel was obsessed with news stories and documentaries about chicle, following the Camden gum imposition. Tonight it was the history of Bubblegum Alley. First-hand accounts of how the walls in the San Luis Obispo alley were decorated with gum, creating blasts of multi-coloured, multi-layered artwork, graffiti. An art historian pointed out that Camden needed to understand the strength of resistance to restrictions on gum, as Bubblegum Alley survived attempts to have its walls cleaned of gum in the 1970s and 1990s.

19

DWAINE SENIOR SAT on the steps at the front of the run-down factory, looking out at his surroundings. He was humming a tune to himself, it sounded revolutionary – a hum likely to cause agitation and uprising in his days in suppressed South Africa.

"Where are Tray and Farooq?" I asked, approaching him on the steps.

"They've left."

"For the day?"

"For good."

"What does that mean?"

"We're alone now."

I didn't like the nonchalant manner in which Dwaine senior was answering my questions. I told him to tell me clearly what was going on. He said I put the kids too close to the source, too close to temptation. He had tried to stop them, but they had taken boxes of gum. They came with other friends. They told Dwaine to tell me that they'd make more money on their own.

I entered the factory with Dwaine senior. I could see evidence of the haste in which the boys had stolen the boxes. I fumed and kicked a box that they had abandoned in their desperate attempt to take as much as they could. They knew any threats I made would be vacuous.

"We can't do this on our own" I said, putting one hand on my temple and massaging it, trying to relieve the sudden stress. Dwaine senior looked up at me confused. He was calm. He took some Biltong, wrapped in cling film, from his inside coat pocket and started to chew it casually.

"Why the panic? They've already made the corrugated stencils. We still have lots of chewing gum left here in the factory. We have all the materials we need."

I removed my hand from my temple, desperately clinging to Dwaine senior's every word. He was now providing me with strength in my moment of weakness – he helped me to re-focus.

"You think this can still work, really?"

"In South Africa I always worked in small units. It made it easier to hide from the Bureau for State Security" he said, neatly wrapping up the now empty cling film and putting it back in his pocket. I stared at him as he chewed the last bit of meat. I couldn't really understand why he was working on this crime with me. His son was sick, hikikomori had a firm grip on him, but Dwaine senior still managed to meet me as requested on time, to plan our attack on the shopping village. I needed to offer him something in return, to demonstrate that I valued his commitment. I thought that showing concern for his son would be a start.

"How is Dwaine junior?"

"I haven't actually seen him. I can't tell for sure."

"You're still talking through walls?"

"He's stopped talking. He slips notes under the door now, requesting food, books and an update on your sabotage operation."

"So he's getting worse?"

"My wife and I leave the things he asks for by the door. When we disappear, he collects them."

Dwaine senior hid his emotions. He talked to me without signs of distress. His uMkhonto we Sizwe experiences had evidently trained him to endure pain and sadness.

"Are you not tempted to seize him when he opens the door?"

"The therapists say that's a bad idea."

"How do you find the strength to come here and help out?"

"His respect for you. He asked me to lend my expertise", Dwaine proudly replied.

"I haven't known your son very long and he's persuaded you to risk everything – you could wind up in prison again."

"We Dubes know good causes. Our criterion for loyalty isn't how long we know someone, but how much we believe in them."

We decided to stay late at the factory to adjust our planning, taking into account the new make-up of the team. We ordered Japanese food and I took a cheap bottle of red wine from my safe, where I'd stashed some of my surveillance equipment. I raised a toast to the operation and to Dwaine junior. Dwaine senior thanked me for toasting his son. He then said that he wanted to play me something. In his isolation, Dwaine junior had become a songwriter. He was writing soulful melancholy. He'd slipped a CD through the gap under his door to his parents – it was a way of letting them into his life without actually letting them in. I looked at the CD in Dwaine senior's sweaty black hand. He held it as if it was a heavy metal – gold. I looked at the CD and, underneath the mixture of fingerprints, there was a permanent marker scribble which read: 'A reply to Mr Green (we don't have to hang)'. I finished a mouthful of Japanese dumpling, took the CD from Dwaine and inserted it into a portable player that I'd found in the factory kitchen. We listened in silence as Dwaine junior stunned us with his silky soul voice.

Let's build up the strength, we've stretched it out a length
I don't know what's next, but we'll stay in touch by text

We don't have to hang (x2)
We don't have to stay, together

Let's dissipate, cause we no longer relate
Let's not be too proud, simply disperse into the crowd

We don't have to hang (x2)
We don't have to stay, together

Let's dissipate, cause we no longer relate
Let's not be too proud, simply disperse into this crowd

We don't have to hang (x2)
We don't have to stay, together

We don't have to hang (x2)
We don't have to stay, together

Dwaine senior left just after midnight. The phone rang: it was the Mayor returning an earlier call. I listened and spoke through the loud speaker. The conversation ended quickly and I finished off the wine, content that I'd persuaded the Mayor to allow me to make the final decisions on the FOGY operation.

20

H E SHOOK MY hand without conviction. He had a loose grip, sceptical eyes and an altogether unsatisfied stance, but before Mathew could question me – much to my delight – we were joined by Christian.

"Congratulations!" he said.

"It was a team effort." I replied as I looked to Mathew, whose eyes were still asking questions.

"You sure it's safe to shut down?", Christian continued. Mathew seized on the opportunity to express his own concerns – stating this was the time to be extra vigilant as the launch of the shopping centre approached. I asked myself why Mathew had to choose now to be insubordinate. I told them both that the Mayor supported disbanding the FOGY task force. He was satisfied that black market consumption of chicle was slowing down in Camden. The Mayor had also instructed that the factory base should remain operational until the opening of the shopping village and that I should personally take on the duty without assistance – to cut costs. Mathew's scepticism turned to pity, self-pity as he saw Christian nod in agreement with me, once the mayor was mentioned and he realised unemployment loomed.

That evening, the run-down factory was converted into a space for celebration. An impromptu event was in full swing to celebrate the success of the FOGY operation and to give the team members a send-off – wishing them well in their common pursuit of jobs in the Foreign Office. There was good attendance from various City Hall departments, including the Design and Development Agency. The men were wearing black tie and the ladies were in elegant dresses. Avril and I were still carrying out our 'relationship on ice' plan, but it didn't stop her from attending the party with Anton. They danced close together when love songs were played. Anton looked handsome (I wasn't too proud to admit it) and the couple were steady on their feet – they danced and were unflinching as they gazed into each other's eyes. I knew that they had something special. Call it low self-esteem or too much pride, but I wasn't going to walk out on her – she'd have to look me in the eyes and say it was over. Anton suddenly moved away from Avril to answer his mobile phone. Christian filled the vacuum. But it appeared that he wasn't a suitable substitute. I'm sure that I saw Avril's neck stretching up, beyond Christian, and then her eyes strained to look through the window, watching Anton's back as he talked on the phone. She disgusted me. I was on ice, and she was on heat – desperate for her new love interest. The night progressed and I was getting desperate for people to leave. Tomorrow was my big day, sabotage day — the eve of the opening. I hadn't made any solid plans with Dwaine senior about the pragmatics of the operation. My phone rang. I retired into one of the offices — the one that I imagined was occupied by the line manager or the quality assurance person back in the live days of the confectionary factory. The office accommodating the person who was important enough to be off the production line, looking at the workers through a glass office, but not important enough to be on the second floor, in an office with closed blinds, working out redundancy packages and calling up mistresses.

"Hello."

"It's Dwaine."

"I was just thinking about you. I haven't finished here. They're still dancing around. Have you got the van?"

"Yes but we need to get together and work through our strategy."

"I won't get away until late now and I need a decent sleep. We'll improvise tomorrow. We have the gum, we have the corrugated plastic stencils and we have a van. We'll be fine!"

"You amateur. Fine! Until tomorrow. Goodnight."

I re-joined the party and witnessed Avril, Anton and Christian leave as a threesome. Avril chose to preserve some dignity for herself — her eyes searched for me through the crowd. They found me, and lovingly penetrated my built-up resistance. I was filled with indecision. I smiled weakly back at her.

At home I couldn't sleep. The magnitude of the next day weighed down on my mind. I needed to switch off, so I switched on the TV and had some *kelewele* and beans. The London regional channel content was predictable – another ode to the Camden gum imposition. This time a well-known TV personality took us through the history of gum. The habit popping up in a number of early civilisations. Ancient Greece forming their gum through mastic tree bark, South Americans used coca leaves – Chinese the Ginseng plant roots, Eskimos used blubber. Ancient Maya and the Aztec had chicle –a natural tree gum. The foundation for sticky, gum–like, substance. I fell to sleep in my armchair as soon as the credits rolled.

21

AT NIGHT CAMDEN was attractively incongruous. Elegantly preserved period houses sat in close proximity to railway bridges that were supported by stale-looking walls. Fly posters of the latest hip hop and indie acts were slapped haphazardly on the bricks. Young tourists dressed in black leather, with black eye-liner and multiple piercings, returned to hostels from heavy-metal gigs. Men in suits and women in dresses floated back from theatres and fancy restaurants, side-stepping the homeless people who were sitting on the floor with shabby dogs and dirt-stained sleeping bags. All of this created the aura of a miscellaneous vanity fair. Dwaine senior and I drove along the back streets of Camden Town to the new shopping village site. We were in a hired blue van with 'Cheap hire transport' written across the side of the vehicle in bold white letters. He was driving too fast for my liking, but I said nothing.

"I met him you know."

"Who?"

"Mandela."

"I see."

"Were together on Robben Island. We were both accused of acting against the state – in the sixties. We shared a conversation or two", he said proudly.

"Yeah great, interesting. You know what you got to do?"

I couldn't keep still; I was lightly tapping my leg with my hand.

"Yes Adrian, I'm an ex-pro."

"You got caught. You spent time in jail."

"I was never caught red handed. I was jailed because I was wrongly accused of being a communist and I was later jailed again for operations that I wasn't involved in."

"So you were jailed on a number of occasions?"

"Not an unlikely thing for a black man in South Africa at the time."

I changed the subject by telling Dwaine senior that he was to be the lookout when we reached the shopping village. He was to stay in the van, while I sabotaged the glass footpaths with gum graffiti. My metal-coated mobile phone rang and vibrated on the van's plastic dashboard, which produced a horrific sound, as the contrasting materials interacted. I picked it up.

"Not now Al, I'm busy!"

"There was an out-of-court settlement with Project Utopia. They offered me twenty grand, but I didn't accept it."

"Your solicitor believes that you can get a better deal in court?"

"No. He said that this is the best financial deal."

"Then why didn't you take it?"

"I wanted a different offer, which they accepted."

"So what was that?"

I dreaded the response.

"I told Project Utopia's lawyers that I wanted the team to be reassembled. The ones who emailed me day and night, pretending to be that New York girl, Helena. They need to keep the dream alive for at least another year, contractually. They agreed, so it's settled. They go live any minute now, so I must be off."

"Take care Al" I said, before ending the call. I couldn't waste energy and time remonstrating with him.

When we got to the site, I jumped out of the van and moved the orange cones that were blocking traffic from entering the road running through the two sides of the shopping village. Dwaine senior then drove through. I ran behind the van until it stopped. I opened the back doors and removed a tub of gum and corrugated plastic stencils. I walked over to the driver's door and told Dwaine senior that I would keep coming down to collect more gum and different stencil designs. I reminded him to be vigilant and to toot the horn if anyone approached. I made my way from the slightly sticky and fresh smelling tarmac to the pavement on my left, and I looked over to the right wing of the complex, which was a mirror image of the left side. The moon shone and the natural light penetrated the middle of the structure: the suspended glass footpaths. They were delectable, and I was mesmerised. I hadn't seen the completed shopping village before. Cables with attached light bulbs were draped between the pillars that were holding up the glass paths. I imagined the lights were lit; there would be romantic walks and proposals on the paths. I had to give it to her, Avril had done a great job. It went against my principle that architecture needed to be for restoration or revolutionary purposes. I made my way up the clear–plastic spiral stairway, which lead up to the glass footpaths and shop entrances. I reached a footpath and I threw the corrugated plastic stencils to the ground, they made a sound that was quick and loud, like a sample play of castanets. I opened the tub of gum, which was mixed with water to make it soft, sticky and easy to paste. I slapped the gum over the stencils, overlapping the carved out letters in my haste. The chicle varied in colour, giving the graffiti a natural urban feel. I felt pleasure when I removed the stencils and the three-dimensional words stood, unaided, as a piece of artwork in their own right. I wished that Dwaine junior, Farooq and Tray could have marvelled at their graffiti, their choice of street lexicon: 'GHETTO WORLD, THE NEW TIP, HOO-DALUMS, DARK CITEE, GUM IZ ERE 2003'. Their words and language were not stuck on filthy walls, but they adorned the fresh glass paths – like artwork in a trendy gallery.

I ran up and down the steps, stocking up on more chicle and changing the stencils, moving along the parallel paths with excitement. By my fifth trip to the van to stock up on gum, Dwaine senior was sleeping. I decided to cut him some slack. At that point, I didn't know that he hadn't locked the door to my office in the factory headquarters, where the monitors were displaying live footage of the footpaths and the complex. Anton, Avril and Christian had made a surprise visit to the factory, with Thai food, maybe because they felt sorry for me being lumbered with the boring task of monitoring the shopping village site. They watched me. Screens were masters of lies and manipulation, so they'd decided that they had to see for themselves. They needed first-hand proof that it was me who was ardently pasting the glass paths, turning the transparent to opaque. I didn't hear the car, the footsteps or the breathing. More importantly, I didn't hear the toot of the horn from our hire car.

"What the hell are you doing?", Christian shouted.

For a split second I was shocked and disorientated by their presence. Then I relaxed, knowing that I had nothing left to lose.

"I'm destroying these fucking bridges, footpaths, whatever you wanna call them … you think you could sack me quietly, low key? I read the emails".

"Adrian", Avril cried.

"Don't you dare, Avril". I said before adding that I wanted my revenge on Anton and Christian, but I chose to wreck the glass footpaths especially because of her. I told her I knew about Anton, the affair. Avril looked at me as if I was a lion cub lost in the world without my mother, with the new resident male honing in on me for the kill.

"Affair? What did this email actually say?"

"It was clear what was going on Avril, don't play games with me now."

"Can you hear yourself, you sound ridiculous, this, what you're doing is just ridiculous?"

I was getting angry that she was trying to put me on the back foot, that she had the temerity to make me justify myself. I continued by telling Avril how I'd read an email about her spending the night around Anton's place. Avril sighed then shouted at me, explaining that Anton's house was practically on the doorstep of our offices and with late nights and early mornings working on the footpath project, it made sense for her to take up the offer of his couch, when the project was at a critical stage. She said if she knew trust and jealousy were issues for me she wouldn't have done so.

"They still wanted to sack me. Did they tell you that?", I retorted. I hadn't quite decided if she was telling the truth, but if it transpired that she was, my cast iron justification for my actions was still the planned sacking. Avril bowed her head and shook it. Christian reached for his phone.

"Enough of this shit, I'm calling the police."

I jumped over the side of the glass footpath that we were standing on, without looking, into the black air. I didn't know or care about the surface that I would meet below, or how far down it was. I landed in an industrial skip and I felt an irregular object against my spine. I quickly established my bearings. Dwaine senior and the van should have been behind me but they weren't. I looked up. Anton's tie was hanging over the side of the footpath, like a pendulum. His face was screwed up and he was shouting, I couldn't hear his words. With my adrenaline pumping, I ran fast into the night. All I could think about was getting my surveillance equipment and leaving the city, the country and the continent.

22

Observation: unclassified 2

> *The words of Ben Jonson seemed apt: 'Fall on me, roof, and bury me in ruin!'. Man can be rash, man can be stupid.*

I RANG AVRIL ON my mobile from my headquarters in the run-down confectionery factory. She answered, but her meek hello was overshadowed by the deafening sounds of police sirens and voices of hysteria.

"It's me."

"Where are you?"

"The factory", I said.

I squinted my eyes and looked through a dirt-smudged window at boys devouring fried chicken from the takeaway opposite.

"You idiot, the police are heading there!"

"Not staying long – just collecting some valuables, stuff I'm planning to sell to a contact I have."

"Don't. I don't want to know. I can't believe what you've done."

"If I could turn back time …"

"You'd better go, don't get caught. Go, bye-bye, go!" Avril said, her voice gradually became quieter. I sensed that someone must have been closing in on her, maybe Anton or a police officer. Her loyalty embarrassed me. I slapped the flip of my phone shut and I looked around the factory, trying to picture where I'd stashed my collection of expensive technology. It was at that moment that I realised I couldn't shift all the gear: I just had to grab the most expensive items. Red lights spun around the factory walls like disco lights: the sound of sirens penetrated my heart. I ducked under a conveyor belt. It was dusty and disused, an item we failed to remove when renovating the factory. There were offish colours on the ground, like dried liquid rust. I wondered how many factory workers had ducked under the conveyor belt when they spotted an approaching line manager, perhaps stuffing into their mouth a chocolate and walnut sweet that was meant to have been wrapped, boxed and ready for distribution. The stakes were higher for me. The sirens and the flashing lights passed by, they were not for me. I continued my search in the dark, too fearful to turn on the lights. I couldn't locate any of the surveillance gear. I heard echoing footsteps. The steps were distinct – I knew them. I could visualise his polished black shoes. He came through the back door. Dwaine stood by me with a look of disgrace upon his face.

"We don't have time. I've loaded the van with your surveillance equipment. Let's get you to the airport."

"How did you know that I would make it?", I said with contempt.

"Instinct."

"You left me there." I said aggressively, and then I realised that I was being too loud and I looked around nervously. Then I shouted again.

"Cool it."

"Cool it?"

"I have a family and a sick son to care for, they need me. I couldn't risk capture – there's been too much capture in my life." Dwaine senior pointed out.

"How long have you been here?"

"I've been here for an hour, making sure that I cleared up all the evidence that is lying around this place. How do you think they got on to us, the kids?"

"The kids were loyal traitors." I replied. I then told Dwaine it was Avril and my bosses; that they had probably come to surprise me with food, keep me company as I carried out remote surveillance of the shopping village. They would have punched in the door code and choked on the takeaway while watching my exploits on the monitor.

AFTERWORD

23

I DIDN'T FOCUS ON the air steward's well-choreographed safety demonstration. My gaze penetrated through his body and into a haze of contemplation. Visions of the Camden fiasco shot through my mind. I'd lost Avril. I remembered her eyes as she stood on the footpath, looking at me with a mixture of contempt and pity. The funny thing about Christian and Anton wanting to sack me was that the reasons they were giving in their emails made sense. I mean, I was proselytising about people not coming up with new ideas or designs but disguising old ones. My job was simply that of a researcher, but I'd clung to the idea that I had a special job, that I was doing something ground-breaking.

I could hear the plane's wheels running along relatively smooth ground and occasional bumps. I swallowed, and my hearing changed. Everything was loud, in stereo sound. The TV screen in the back of the patterned chair in front of me was small. My eyes were working hard to focus on the film that was showing. Maybe Pacita was right; maybe we will change to be more compatible with technology. Then I asked myself why we needed to further embrace it. The power of technology had destroyed Al. It had left him wanting and needing technology like an addictive drug.

I awoke from a sleep. My second full sleep on the plane. I looked out of the window and I checked the journey update channel on the in-flight TV. We had just passed Miami. I was more excited by the fact that I had reached page 700 of my book than the prospect of living in El Salvador and meeting up with Mr Lopez at the airport. I skimmed over the words and sentences of the last two paragraphs. I tried to skip ahead and peep at the last word. I felt guilty: why the rush? I'd struggled through 699 pages and now I was cheating – I was cheating myself. I started from the top of the page. I read meticulously and then I closed the book at the end and drank the wine left over from my in-flight meal. I threw a stick of gum into my mouth and I waited for the plane to land.

Acknowledgements

I WOULD LIKE TO thank my family for their encouragement (Mum, Melissa, Yvonne, Kofi Jr, Kwasi, Dad, Claudia and whole family and friends). Also Claire Daley for her editorial input, Donna Dalby for helping with earlier versions.

Adrian Sarpong works for the mayor – as a Community Observer. His mind has become troubled. He ponders why fresh, new designs are lacking from society when technology allows for so much more than recycled ideas. Adrian is also troubled by the impact of the internet on his friend Al, his duplicitous employers and cheating girlfriend. *Modern Mania* explores prevalent early 21st century themes – including the manipulation of consumer products for terror and our ambivalent relationship with the internet.

Printed in the United States
By Bookmasters